URBAN FOLKCORE

NICK JONES

*"Do not go gentle into that good night.
Rage, rage, against the dying of the light"*
Dylan Thomas

AL TARRAGONA

y mensajes al 627/73 97 81

TOROS - Murcia

[illegible] 12 de octubre

RE 22:04

[illegible]

ONE

October 31st, 1996 – 7 PM

The sky over Ghostward was a bruise, swollen and heavy with the promise of rain. Beneath it, the four-story concrete parking lot lay like an abandoned relic, its edges softened by grime, walls stained from decades of pollution and neglect. A pale streetlamp flickered near the entrance, casting a weak light onto two parked vehicles outside. One, an unmarked black sedan. The other, a van bearing the words GPD CRIME SCENE UNIT.

The fourth floor stretched out in cavernous silence. Cement walls absorbed faint noises from the city below, trapping the interior in an unnatural stillness. Two figures stood inside, shifting on their heels near an open elevator shaft. Their shadows stretched long and dark, jagged against the dusty floor. Detective Malone, a silver-haired brute with thick sausage lips, gripped his cigarette between his teeth. The faint cherry glow of its tip punctuated the gloom. Beside him, his partner, Granger, cracked his neck in discomfort. Granger's pencil moustache twitched compulsively. A common side effect of his looming paranoia. Malone watched as the man tugged at his shirt collar, his body radiating unease. The air was sharp around them both, filled with the mingling scent of mildew and death. It clung to the skin like an unwelcome touch.

Both men stared upwards.

The body hung above them like a human chandelier, a grotesque display of flesh swaying gently in the stagnant air. The ropes that held him in position, Malone noted, seemed to trail upwards. They disappeared through an area of collapsed ceiling, likely secured to an old metal beam somewhere above. The corpse was nude. An overweight, middle-aged man. His arms splayed into a mocking T – a deliberate and callous pose meant to evoke the crucifixion in the minds of onlookers. Atop his slack, balding head, a crown rested, fashioned from bleached animal bones and haphazardly bound with cheap twine. Despite the grisly spectacle, a subtle dimple lingered on the man's left cheek – a fragile echo of his humanity, or perhaps a final defiant smile in the face of death. Had he known his killer? Had he sensed what was coming? Or, in some tragic twist of fate, had he embraced his end with open arms?

Malone scowled at the corpse as if owed money or an explanation, but it would give him neither. The cuts across its flesh were shallow and deliberate. They crisscrossed the man's pallid skin, covering him almost from head to toe. Fresh blood glistened under the harsh yellow floodlights positioned by the Crime Scene Unit only moments earlier. Having hung yellow tape around the scene, they were busy now, recording their findings out on the street below. The victim's stomach – round and engorged – seemed to have suffered from a hastily stitched surgical procedure. Dark, uneven sutures held it together, though it oozed with deep infection.

Malone studied the scene quietly. There was something ancient about it. Profane. A tableau plucked from a long forgotten corner of hell, deposited here, inside this urban tomb.

"Goddamn devil worshippers," he muttered, flicking ash onto the blood-streaked floor. He took another long drag on his cigarette, his gaze unwavering.

"Guessing he aint got ID on him," Granger replied, squinting at the corpse. He snorted, then shifted on the balls of his feet. "Saw a gang of gutterpunks holed up down the road a couple nights back. Could be we drag 'em in. Pin it on one or two. Crack some deserving commie skulls."

Malone ignored him, waving his words aside. Details began to emerge in the wounds as he studied them. At first, the cuts seemed random. But then, slowly, surely, they revealed themselves. There were runes, pentacles, and other strange symbols carved with precision into the man's flesh. A drop of blood trembled on the bridge of his nose. Fat and crimson, it surrendered to gravity, striking the car park with a faint splatter.

Malone exhaled slowly, running a hand through his greying hair. He'd had enough of this shit. It seemed to be happening every few weeks now. Strange events. None of them making any sense. Last month, a thief had somehow walked horizontally along the side of the Derleth high-rise, raiding a locked penthouse and escaping in an impossible matter of minutes. At first, the GPD had assumed the culprit used a grappling hook, but eyewitness reports and security footage told a far stranger tale. The figure had moved smoothly upwards, unsupported and unharnessed – gravity be damned. Then there was the case just last week: a man found stabbed to death inside a locked room, the murder weapon lodged in the ceiling high above his body. What's more, the victim had used his final moments to scrawl a message on the walls in his own blood:

THEY'RE COMING! THEY'RE COMING!
THEY'RE COMING!
THEY'RE HERE.

Yep, Malone missed the old days, that was for sure. Back when Ghostward was easy, its criminals dumb as rocks, and things like gravity and reason still applied. His cigarette hung loosely from his lips, the ash at its tip threatening to fall. Malone's shoulders sagged, resolve seeping from him like an old boiler losing steam. He closed his eyes, imagining briefly the night he could have had. As the sun began to set, he'd arrive at his ex-wife's house on Elmrose Place to take Danny trick-or-treating. She'd smile politely, thank him, and head out to dance at a club downtown. But that wasn't meant to be. Not anymore. He opened his eyes.

Malone fixated on the body above, his mind trying to piece together the ritualistic mess of it all. A sudden presence behind him made him flinch. He turned – a woman stood there, heels clicking softly against stone. Where the hell had she come from?

"Ghostward's boys in blue," she said, her voice dripping with disdain. "First to arrive, last to understand a goddamn thing."

Her tone was thick, layered with hidden meaning. Turning to face her, Malone couldn't tell if it was pity, annoyance, or a joke. Whatever she meant, the woman was unexpected, and unwelcome. At a glance, she seemed to be a simple citizen of Ghostward, dressed in blue denim jeans and a stylish brown overcoat stopping just below her waist. Her hair was the color of spun gold tossed with dirt. She'd tied it back in a neat ponytail. Her shoes were durable and impeccably clean. What's more, they were fashionable. Malone was sure he'd seen those exact shoes in a department store at Wescott Plaza only recently. He remembered because Sarah wanted a pair.

"On my salary?" he'd asked teasingly, not meaning anything by it. Later that afternoon when they got home and had sent Danny out to play, she'd asked for a divorce.

Here, now, in this place, Malone saw the shoes as a symbol. And this strange woman – she was the hidden orchestrator of his marriage's demise. He knew it wasn't true, but he needed somebody to hate. He needed somebody to blame.

As the woman spoke, Malone leered. Who the hell was she? A tourist? Surely not local. Most Ghost-wardians knew better than to mess with the GPD, let alone trek through one of their crime scenes. Yet here she was. No doubt, some college-educated bitch who thought she could save the world. Malone glanced over at his partner, who was itching to remind the stranger of where she stood. He'd put her in her place.

"Who the fuck are you?" Granger demanded, jabbing a bony finger in her face. The woman didn't flinch. In fact, she barely blinked. This pissed him off more. Reaching into her jacket pocket, she smiled at them both. Ignoring the question as she removed a soft pack of Lucky Strikes, she placed one between her lips.

"It's Detective Granger, right?"

Her question was rhetorical, and she followed it up with a: "Still as vitriolic as ever, I see." Pausing, she tucked the pack away and drew a Zippo lighter, bringing its flame to her face, sheltering it with her hand from a light wind billowing in from outside.

"We've met before, detectives. You just don't remember." She blew a thick cloud into their faces. Granger waved it away with a furious swipe of his hand. Malone took it, letting the warm smoke roll over him. "You're about to forget this encounter as well." She continued.

Unable to contain himself any longer, Malone stepped forward.

"Now listen here, lady..." he began, "you're interfering with an official police investi—"

"Stop," the woman interrupted. Holding up her free hand for both detectives to see, she twisted her fingers into an unusual gesture, clasping her thumb, index and pinkie together, whilst raising her middle and ring high. Pointing the palm of her hand in their direction, she closed her eyes, as if falling into deep meditation. Immediately, her hand seemed to ignite, crackling with an ethereal lavender glow. As the flickering blades of energy rose before them, the detectives minds became wrapped in a warm, syrupy haze. An inexplicable calm descended on them as their anger and confusion was swallowed whole. Slumping forward, their eyes glazed over. Their bodies swayed, caught in the tide of some new, dominating emotion. Deep down, in the recesses of their skulls, they still bubbled with rage, but this new sensation was a commanding force. It overrode their native state with unnerving clarity. The two men groaned, their voices dreary and dull.

"Now, off you go," the woman said, as if she were a parent speaking to a toddler. Helpless against this invading calm, the detectives didn't even realize they'd been dismissed. In their minds, they were still playing cops and robbers as the city's true threats watched silently from the shadows.

With the detectives gone, the glow atop the woman's hand spluttered out into nothing. She sighed heavily, both exhaustion and sadness fighting for control. The bravado she'd expressed only moments earlier seemed to be little more than a front. The Esternati were unravelling, and each fraying thread pulled against her chest – a noose cinching tighter with each passing second. Her cigarette slipped from her lips, bouncing off the toe of her shoe. She pressed her palms to her temples, doubling over as the fatigue clawed its way inside.

"…everything…" she whispered softly, "…everything… spinning… again…"

◉◉◉

Rain fell in heavy sheets. It hammered the pavement, ricocheting against the faded awning of a small laundromat nestled between the crumbling buildings of downtown Ghostward. The sign above the entrance buzzed warmly despite the downpour. Its purple neon letters stood defiantly against the storm. *The Midnight Laundromat – 24/7*. Beneath those words, a cheerful cartoon logo flickered in rhythmic loops. A personified bottle of washing detergent twirled and danced alongside a smiling coffee mug. A quirky detail that stood out against the otherwise grim backdrop.

It was 10 PM. The neighbouring shops had closed hours ago. But this was the laundromat's busiest period. The door creaked as it opened, letting in a rush of cold, moist air from outside. Within its long, narrow space, the atmosphere was dim but functional, lit by a row of flickering fluorescent lights overhead. The tiled floor was scuffed and stained from years of hurried foot traffic, the walls, once a vibrant yellow, now faded and peeling.

Several machines stood in two ordered rows at the center of the laundromat, their glass doors fogged with condensation. From somewhere deeper inside, a tinny radio played "It's All Coming Back To Me Now" by Celine Dion. A solitary vending machine lay against the back wall, its brightly lit compartments containing ancient cans of soda, forever unwanted. A faint whir filled the air, blending with the occasional drip of rainwater leaking through cracks in the ceiling. Outside, the neon aura of the laundromat's sign reflected off the wet pavement, casting ephemeral streaks of light against the front window.

Three patrons currently occupied the laundromat, each absorbed in their own routine. A woman, hunched over one of the machines, sorted through a bundle of damp clothes. On a nearby bench, an older gentleman sat with his arms crossed, his gaze fixed on the spin of his washing through the steaming porthole. On the other side of the store, a younger man – barely in his twenties – methodically withdrew clean underpants from a dryer, folding each into a tidy pile in a plastic basket he'd brought along.

A bell rang as the doors opened. The woman who had only hours earlier disrupted a police investigation entered. Her dark brown coat now appeared almost black as it dripped with water. Stepping inside, she flicked stray locks from her eyes with a toss of her head.

Nobody looked up. Weaving through the building, she made her way to the vending machine at the back. Once there, the woman placed her hand against the machine's heavily scratched glass. A silver ring on her finger caught the lights above. It revealed a small insignia, embossed with the shape of a lavender flower.

Looking over her shoulder, she scanned the room. Still unnoticed. *Good,* she thought. Returning to her mission, the woman traced the shape from her ring against the glass. Instantly, the machine faded, becoming ephemeral, translucent, phantasmagorical. She passed quietly through the illusion. It solidified behind her with the faintest of clicks, depositing the woman into a dark passageway that descended beneath the earth.

She moved quickly; her footsteps swallowed by the damp hush of the tunnel. It stretched beneath Ghostward like an arterial wound. A secret path carved through the rotting underbelly of the city. Rusted pipes trembled along the ceiling, pulsing with the distant throb of bass-heavy music from the streets above – a muffled *VROOM VROOM VROOM* pressing through layers of stone. Phosphorescent mosses clung to the brickwork, revealing patches of black mould and sections of graffiti, spraypainted with erratic hands. Ahead of her, something shifted out of sight – a metal grate shuddering in protest as wind funnelled through it from above.

Below ground, the Esternati Chapter House remained unseen, occulted within the city's pallid ribs like its forgotten heart. Dust-choked lightbulbs warmed her path, their wavering light guiding her along it. After several minutes, she reached a dead end. Here, a gleaming stainless steel door stood against the surrounding grime. Its polished surface reflected her form like an eerie doppelgänger trapped within the depths. Beside it, a small security panel stuck out from the brickwork. She punched in a passcode, stepped back, and waited as the door slid open.

Emerging into a sprawling, subterranean office, the woman ran her fingers through her hair and listened. Low voices murmured beneath the rhythmic clatter of keyboards and shuffling of parchment. A cacophony of digital chirps and mechanical wails tore occasionally through the office – high-pitched beeps clashing with guttural static as dial-up modems fought for a foothold in the world wide web. Buzzing CRT screens illuminated the room artificially. Desks cluttered the office, each heaped with ancient scrolls and leather-bound books. Their covers, inscribed with magical sigils and strange titles, whispered ominously of secret and forbidden things. On the far wall, a medieval tapestry hung, its colors pleasantly vivid despite its obvious age. The artwork depicted an army of winged figures moving through the skies, each locked in an eternal war with monstrous and writhing entities, too large and too wrong to be named. A rolling green meadow stretched beneath the battle, untouched by the carnage. It established a horizon, providing an uncommon sense of depth.

Around her, men and women – most dressed in suits – poured over the obscure texts on their desks, intermittently gossiping amongst themselves.

"Speak for yourself, Richard," a thirty-something woman with a large scar across her chin said jovially. "You even get a glimpse of the man? Huge! Took five of us just to get him down the stairs!"

Her colleague, an older man with a scruffy grey beard, peered sardonically over the top of his glasses. Turning in his chair, he chuckled. "Come on, Darlene, it can't have been that bad! Remember the gibbering mass of F'thagnan last year? That was a goddamn trial."

A third man, busy fixing Polaroid photos to a sprawling evidence board, glanced up at the two. "Gibbering mass of F'thagnan? You've been reading too much Lovecraft."

"Hey, Howard had his issues, but I'll be damned if he didn't get some things right," Richard replied with a glint in his eyes.

As the woman weaved through the main chamber, the man at the evidence board spotted her and offered a friendly smile. "Sam! Can't keep you away!"

"Couldn't sleep after the day I've had," she replied.

The man paused, mentally moving through several filing cabinets in his mind. "Yeah, graphic stuff alright. Body's all cleaned up now though, if you fancy a late-night autopsy."

"Thanks, Xavier. Exactly what the doctor ordered."

"You just missed the Comandante by the way," he mentioned as Sam turned away. "Rushed out of here like his ass was on fire."

"Knowing David, he probably ate some bad take-away," she joked.

Turning away, Sam left the main chamber behind. She stopped in front of a side door labelled, in bold black letters: POST-MORTEM EXAMINATION. Pushing it open, she entered.

This room was much smaller. At its heart, a stainless steel slab. The cadaver from the parking garage now lay atop it, pale and motionless. In the clinical light, Sam could see now subtle details that the parking lot had disguised. Uneven stubble along the man's jawline. A wine-red, mottled birthmark above his left ear. A faded tan line circling one finger. A wedding ring, perhaps? Her colleagues had done a good job of tidying him up. The wounds were cleaned, causing them to appear even more red and raw in the cold white lustre. Against the left-hand wall, the animal bone crown had been set aside for later examination.

Closing the door behind her, Sam began to change into medical scrubs and gloves. Once prepared, she picked up a clipboard. Pressing it loosely against her chest, she retrieved a portable tape recorder with her other hand. Taking a deep breath, she turned to face the slab. A tray of neatly organized surgical instruments gleamed at the ready nearby.

Raising the recorder to her mouth, she clicked it and began.

"Autopsy conducted by Compatriota Samantha Lockart at the Esternati[1] Ghostward Chapter House. The date is October 31st, 1996. Subject is a white male, likely mid-to-late forties. Cause of death, currently unknown."

Moving around the victim, Sam started to examine his wounds.

"The body is covered in many superficial cuts. Perhaps from a scalpel or other fine blade."

A pause.

"Cuts appear to be inscriptions."

She leaned in closer, trying to make out the intended shapes in the thousands of tiny slashes.

---

1 **The Esternati** – An ancient Order dedicated to defending humanity against supernatural threats from the Astral Plane. Believed to have originated somewhere around the Mediterranean, their name means "those who have been put outside." For much of their existence, they were a revolutionary and radical force against evil. In recent years, they have grown fat, complacent, and bureaucratic in their approach.

"Cuneiform. On the left pectoral region – spells from Mesopotamia."

Moving down the same side, her fingers traced the air over the corpse's ribs, careful not to touch the skin.

"Left lateral thorax - Ogham script[2]. Invocations common in many Druidic traditions." Sam knew their overlapping twig-shaped symbols well. She'd written her dissertation on the language back in her early twenties. Even now, those scholarly instincts were vibrating, a curious excitement for the mystery at hand.

"These don't belong here," she said. "Not geographically. Not thematically either."

Sam's stomach churned. Her eyes drifted lower, stopping just above the man's penis, homing in on a series of organized cuts beneath his belly button. She exhaled sharply.

"And now a hymn to Kali? Carved into the suprapubic region. Favoured by the Aghori[3] sect."

Shocked, Sam took a step back, resisting the urge to stroke her chin thoughtfully and ruin the sterility of her gloves.

---

2 *Ogham Script* – *An ancient alphabet found on Old Welsh stone monuments. It was used in Ireland and parts of the United Kingdom from the 4th to the 10th century CE. Also known as the Celtic Tree Alphabet, as letters are named after trees and resemble twigs.*

3 *Aghori Sect* – *Hindu devotees of the goddess Shiva who are famed for their macabre religious practices such as smearing cremated ashes on their bodies, drug usage, and consumption of human flesh, among other things.*

"This isn't just a single ritual… It's a mosaic." Her brow furrowed. "It's as if every cult in Ghostward had something to gain from this man's sacrifice…"

It didn't make any sense. The carvings were all wrong. Careless. Amateur, even. It was like the killer had a wide knowledge of the occult, but none of the depth required for any true ceremonial magic. Setting that mystery aside, Sam returned to the victim's stomach – to the poorly stitched gash across his abdomen. As she peeled back the blackened sutures with the edge of her scalpel, the wound parted reluctantly, revealing raw tissue underneath. Festering pus and the stink of rot wafted up from the wound.

"Subject presents with evidence of a poorly devised surgical procedure to the upper abdomen. Performed antemortem. The wound is approximately one week old, with clear signs of infection. Whoever did this wasn't concerned for his health."

Placing the scalpel down on the steel tray beside her, Sam began to pace the room slowly. The tape recorder remained in her free hand as she walked. Her mind was a tornado, swirling and churning through potential possibilities. Each one was disturbing, but some more so than others.

"So," Sam began, stopping mid-stride. "He was cut open, stitched back up, and then used as somebody's personal Grimoire…" Her pacing resumed. "But why? And by who?"

These questions hung around her like threads of a spider's web as she returned to the slab. Gripping the dead man's right ankle with one hand, she lifted it up to her face for a better look. Blood-streaked symbols were carved there, too. Those, however, were smaller – easy to miss. They were also far more intricate, almost elegant in their design. A lump began to rise in her throat. Connections were forming in her mind, and she wasn't sure she liked where they were headed.

"Initial hypothesis…" she said into the recorder. "The surgical wound, along with the symbols on the subject's ribs, chest and pubic region appear to…" Sam paused, swallowing the lump. "…serve as camouflage, reflecting a blend of… *contradictory* traditions. The symbols on the right ankle, however, are… interesting, to say the least. Perhaps they are the true focal point of our killer's ritual?"

Setting the ankle back down, Sam adjusted the overhead light, directing its beam onto the unassuming carvings across the man's feet. Illuminated, complex, and inscribed impossibly small. Recognition bloomed inside her mind.

"Pahlavi script! Middle Persian.[4] These refer to the *Yazdān mayt* – the morbid angels of Borborite Gnosticism…"

She hesitated.

____

4 **Pahlavi Script/Middle Persian** – The written language of Persia (now Iran) used between the 2nd Century BCE to the 7th.

"Only two groups in the entire country would know these exact words… Either the Esternati have a killer in our midst, or… the *Altiorem*[5] did this."

With that dangerous answer now in the open, Sam's fingers hovered over her tray of surgical instruments. The scissors. Their smooth metal was cold against her rubber glove, chilling her skin.

"Beginning my internal examination."

Positioning herself over the body, Sam prepared to remove the remainder of the stitching across the man's gut.

"Argument against current theory." Her voice was more even now, though still alarmed. "The Altiorem Cult has shown no sign of hostility in over a decade. Esternati consensus is they're too busy playing Illuminati to get their hands dirty like this."

"And yet… those symbols come from a very specific source. You can't just grease the palms of some Street Witch or Gutter Prophet to learn them."

Pulling on one of the threads, she held it up to her eye.

"Catgut stitches in the abdomen. Retrieving a sample for further analysis."

She carefully placed it in a small evidence bag, then returned with her scissors to the next suture. A faint

---

5 **The Altiorem** – A prominent cult in the city of Ghostward. Originally known as *The Mortuum Altiorem*, meaning "superior corpse" in Latin. There was a time not long ago in which they were the primary antagonists of The Esternati Order.

flicker of motion beneath the skin caught her eye. Her breath hitched. Beneath the pendulous flesh, something shifted. Subtle. But unmistakable. A ripple on the surface of a lake, disturbed by a lurking predator below.

Sam's pulse quickened. She tightened her grip on the surgical scissors, fighting a growing instinct to pull back and run. The bulge pressed outwards, stretching through the pale flesh in a macabre display. Deliberate. Persistent.

Alive.

"What the…?"

The bulge swelled, the skin struggling to contain whatever was inside. A faint, almost imperceptible heat radiated from the remains, causing the air around it to distort and bend. Sam's eyes widened.

"Something's moving… Something on the inside…"

The body detonated in a thunderous burst of blood and fire. A deafening roar tore through the room. Black tentacles lashed out towards her. Green flames belched from the suction cups on each appendage. They flared like furnace vents.

Sam fell back, shielding her face from the splatter of blood and gore. The walls caught and ignited. Smoke filled the air. Acrid. Suffocating. She coughed violently. Her vision blurred.

Before she could react, one of the tentacles reached her. Coiling itself around her torso with terrifying speed, it seared through her clothes. Sam screamed. Her feet left the ground. The slithering arm lifted her, slammed her effortlessly against a wall. She tried to gasp. There was nothing left to breathe. Her lungs seized. Desperate for oxygen. Every inhale a strangled and burning knot. The writhing, dark muscle constricted her ribcage. Inside, something popped and cracked. Bones splintering painfully.

Screams rang out from the offices beyond, familiar voices twisting into raw, animalistic howls. The spreading inferno had reached them. The door to the examination room burst open. A figure stumbled in through the blaze. Xavier. He tugged and pulled at his flaming clothes in a panic. A second tentacle shot towards him like a whip-crack. His head jerked sideways. His lower jaw wrenched clean off. His face shredded into thick, bloody ribbons. He crumpled without a word, swallowed instantly by the emerald fire.

"No!" Sam choked out, thrashing against the creature's grip. It was beyond strong – beyond anything she'd ever imagined. The *Yazdān mayt* were supposed to be powerful, but this? This was godlike. Impossible. Her ribs groaned. Dark spots swarmed her sight, the world around her tilting away. Muffled noises. Distant heat. Pain exploding behind her eyeballs. Her mind flooding with static.

This is it, she thought.

This is how I die…

The Discord, Lower East End, 11 PM…

The hardcore venue boomed with sound and fury. Perched on the corner of Maine Street and Cinder Way, it stood as a defiant pulse against the traffic that barrelled urgently through the rain. A neon sign at the building's front lit the pavement with an eerie hue. A flashing arrow hung beneath, pointing down a dark, graffiti-plastered alley to where the entrance lay. Beneath the narrow awning on the street out front, small groups lingered – hoods pulled low over sharp haircuts, denim jackets patched and fraying at the seams. The faces of some shadowed by the brims of soaking baseball caps. Others lit by the sparking of plastic lighters against home-rolled smokes. Black boots scuffed the wet pavement. Inked knuckles peeked out from fingerless gloves, rapping restless rhythms against thighs. Some shared watery beers, others drew thick black X's on their hands with Sharpies, watching their intoxicated counterparts with judging stares. Jock moshers stretched out their limbs, preparing themselves for the night. Three Krishnacore kids huddled nearby, speaking prayers in hushed tones. Out of sight, a cluster of skinheads plotted how best to slip inside unnoticed. For some, it would be a walk in the park. For those flaunting swastika tattoos, entry would be hard-won.

Inside the venue's pink brick walls, the air was thick with sweat and sound. Carnage reigned over the center of the room, where a mosh pit churned with relentless, violent energy. Flickering jack-o-lanterns lined the elevated stage in celebration of the season, their triangular eyes and toothy grins casting malevolent shadows across the crowd.

Onstage, Hunter Garcia, frontman of *The Outrage*, stomped back and forth, microphone in hand. Sweat streaked down his exposed biceps, mingling with the grime still clinging from the night before. A tattoo of a slobbering bulldog peeked out from the neckline of his drenched white singlet, hinting at a larger work etched across his sternum. His voice tore through the Discord, guttural and raw, but his focus was on the pit. He drew energy from the swarm.

Hunter recognized the moshers below him like old scars. That shirtless dude windmilling in the center? Every scene had one. Angry and flailing, a figure more concerned with violence than release. Hunter had seen a hundred of them over the years. They all thought they were tough shit. They all fundamentally missed the point.

At the back of the stage, Raj, their guitarist swung his instrument with reckless abandon. His movements were kinetic. Each riff played, a declaration of revolution. Hunter loved the guy, but lately... He grimaced. Raj owed him five grand – a "slight" gambling problem that had gotten out of control on tour, somewhere between Chicago and Philly.

In the crowd, the shirtless man surged forward, swinging his fists in wide, vicious arcs, clearing a path through the melee. A young woman in a faded hoodie launched herself sideways, sending vibrations through the other dancers. She threw a punch, channelling it downwards, trying to split the earth.

An instrumental bridge afforded Hunter time to breathe. Pulling his eyes away from the audience, he turned to face Mikey, their drummer, perched at the back of the stage. Crashing cymbals cut through the noise. Mikey was younger than the rest of them – barely out of high school. But he knew his shit, and Hunter – not a natural-born musician – relied on him to stay on tempo. Mikey was rad, but the kid cycled through girlfriends like setlists. A different doe-eyed beauty on his arm each show. A trail of broken hearts in his wake.

One of those hearts belonged to Kim, who said she was fine, but Hunter still worried. There she was now, her heavy bassline hitting the audience like a body blow. Kim was a riot of color – a kaleidoscope of shredded tartan and ocean-blue fishnets. Her crimson hair blazed under the stage lights. A careful selection of band patches dotted her vest like stars. *The Misfits, Converge, Agnostic Front, Rage Against The Machine, Nirvana.* In a way, Kim was the lifeblood of the band. She was altruistic, still believing music could change the world. Hunter envied her. Where was his hope? The passion he'd had when he'd founded the band? Had he lost it somewhere along the way? If so, it was probably buried under miles of road and nights just like this, where the music was increasingly dwarfed by a growing apathy.

Within the swirling dry ice smoke, Kim's instrument orbited her body, almost moving with a will of its own. She sprinted across the stage, raising her bass high, then swinging it down, her rainbow-painted fingernails scratching against the trembling strings.

Back out in the crowd, a teenager spun on one foot, extending his leg and arcing it through his friends in a wide and deliberate kick. The force sent another ripple through the throng, driving others briefly away, before they rushed in again. Reaching into the ring of people surrounding the mosh, the teen grabbed his date's hand, pulling her towards him, emboldening her to join in. The newcomer, dressed in a faded *Sick Of It All* shirt, darted out, her arms flailing as her elbows and shoulders collided with anyone in reach. On the edge of the circle, a pair of friends shoved each other hard, laughing maniacally as they were swallowed up by a wave of bodies.

Planting his boot on the foldback speaker and leaning out over the crowd, Hunter brought his mic to his face and tore through the air with a dominating scream.

"THEY WANT YOU MUMMIFIED!"

He paced the edge of the stage, then, with a sudden burst, he marched toward the crowd.

"THEY WANT YOU CATATONIC! THEY WANT YOU PARALYZED..."

He held his microphone out overhead for the headbangers up front to jump in on:

"THEY WANNA CONTROL THE MARKETS!"

Raising their middle fingers high, the audience fell into a trance, a breakdown lurching and rearing its ugly head. The pit convulsed into a whirlpool of human flesh, powered by the intimidating growls and frantic shrieks of crunchy guitars.

Hunter didn't hesitate. Clambering atop the Marshall amp next to Raj, he launched himself from the stage. For a moment, he was gone – swallowed by the undulating mass, the weight of the crowd crushing the breath from his chest – until light and air returned, and Hunter surfaced again from the eye of the storm.

The pit froze for a silent heartbeat – a ring of bodies holding tension like a tightly drawn bow. It poised and teetered, then, like an arrow loosed, someone charged into the void. The circle collapsed in on itself, consumed once more in an eruption of adrenaline.

In the midst of it, somebody stumbled, nearly losing their balance in the rotation. A hand shot out, yanking them upright, pulling them away from the trampling of feet. No words passed between the two – only a fleeting moment of solidarity before both disappeared back into the mosh.

On the other side of the venue, leaning casually against the bar, Jessie DeLuca watched with a bemused smile. She sipped from a plastic cup, her dark eyes following Hunter as he returned to the band. She wondered how he did it—how he withstood the heat. Jessie had shared the stage with that dickhead many times, her sweat catching in her thick brown dreadlocks. But to leap into the pit, which seemed to burn with the very fires of hell? With her tattered maroon jeans and heavy leather jacket, Jessie was sure she'd die from heatstroke. And no. There was no way she was changing her get-up. She had a reputation to uphold after all.

The song transitioned again, moving into its home stretch. Hunter took another running jump, casting himself as hard as he could across the sea of raised hands. Surfing through tattooed arms and studded bracelets, his voice rang out with furious desperation as the extended mic lead tangled itself around his torso.

"FACING MONSTERS IN THE MOONLIGHT! GUESS THE FIRE MAKE IT ALRIGHT! MARCHING STREETS FOR THE REAL FIGHT! GOT THE FASCISTS IN MY RED SIGHT! CUT AWAY THE CANCER BLIGHT! GUILLOTINE PROVIDING INSIGHT! DROP A NAZI, TAKE YOUR BIRTH RIGHT! ROCK N' ROLL, WHERE THE TEETH BITE!"

Above it all, Hunter grinned now like a man possessed. *There it is. There's my spark*, he thought. *Not lost quite just yet.* The sensation, both familiar and new, crackled through him like an old friend. An embodiment of raw, unfiltered resistance. His words, a violent expression of solidarity for the outcasts, for the forgotten. He understood it all again. He'd entered the zone. To be here tonight was to surrender—to the music, to the movement, and mostly importantly, to belonging.

▣▣▣

Sometime later, after the show was done and the venue had begun to empty out, Jessie remained. At the bar, she sat on a stool, her back to the thinning crowd. Her fingers traced the edge of her cup idly. In front of her, the bartender wiped down the counter, sliding fresh drinks to the last lingering patrons. The faint smell of spilled beer, soda and sweat hung around her, mixing with the hushed tones of conversation and clinking glass.

Hunter approached from behind, his canvas Vans scuffing softly against the worn floorboards. He was still riding high from his performance, his shoulder-length curly hair, stained by a home-job bleaching, hung tangled and damp with sweat. It clung to his angular face. A grin tugged at his lips, framed by his sharp jawline and high cheekbones. Two large black plugs were suspended in his stretched-out ear lobes. His lean frame, in combination with these other features, gave him an air of both boyish innocence and unpredictable ferality. Closing in on Jessie, the wild intensity in his deep brown eyes softened.

"Buy you a drink, *amiga*?" he asked, his voice slightly croaky from the performance.

Jessie didn't turn. Her fingers continued to stroke the sides of her cup. "Already taken care of," she replied.

Sliding onto the stool next to her, Hunter leaned against the bar. "How're you doing, Jessie?" His tone was quieter now. Probing instead of cocky.

Jessie swivelled in her chair, her dark green eyes meeting his. She gave him a small smile. There was a stiffness to it. An edge of discomfort. Part of her had been hoping to avoid this conversation, but something else made her stay.

"What do you want, Hunter?" she asked wearily.

Hunter threw his hands up in mock defence, his carefree demeanour returning. "*¡Oye!* You came to my show! I'm just being polite."

The bartender slid a bottle of beer his way. He caught it with ease. Hunter let the silence continue as he took a swig. Placing the bottle down, he added, "…to the girl who broke my heart."

Jessie let out a quiet laugh despite herself. She shook her head. For all his theatrics, Hunter's self-effacing humour had always found a way to break through her shell. There was history between them. Complicated, sure, but not all bad.

"Well…" Her voice softened. "I'm still standing, aren't I?"

Hunter raised his beer in a toast. His presence warm. Genuine. Encouraged by her reply, he said, "Here's to you, Jessie DeLuca." He chuckled.

"Back at ya." Jessie lifted her cup to meet his. She sipped at the remaining dregs. "How's Kim working out for you guys?"

Hunter nudged her shoulder playfully with his own. "Why? You jealous? Miss being in the band?"

"Pfft, please," Jessie scoffed, her cheeks flushing red. "It's been two years. Seems like it's going well."

"Well, you did recommend her, y'know..." He trailed off. Old memories threatened to emerge. Things left unspoken. "Hey!" he exclaimed suddenly, reaching for something in his jeans pocket. He pulled out a small, crumpled flyer and tried to smooth it out on the counter. Sliding it beneath her nose, he said, "We're playing again next week. You should come. Bring Elijah." Hunter paused. "How is he anyway?"

Jessie prickled. She'd not thought about her brother for some time. She loved the guy – he was her twin, after all – but Elijah was sick in the head, and that sickness had infected their whole life. Eventually, their father had convinced her Elijah needed more help than they could give him. It'd been tough, but her brother was in a place now that could actually help him. Elijah had hated them for it. They'd maintained radio silence ever since.

"Give it a rest, will you, Garcia?"

The tension between the two of them flared. It wasn't enough to break the moment, but it was palpable all the same. Jessie took the flyer absent-mindedly, folding it in half and tucking it into her jacket without a word. Hunter watched with longing building in his heart.

▓▓▓
◉◉◉

Midnight...

The rain outside still hadn't let up. Neither had the nightlife. Masked trick-or-treaters danced down the grimy city streets, their laughter and mischievous shouting blending with the sounds of rushing cars and tooting horns. Pedestrians hunched themselves against the weather. Some clutched umbrellas, others appeared resigned to the downpour.

David turned a corner, moving with purpose. He had an aged but studious face, drawn together with concern. Seeing the teenage trick-or-treaters up to no good ahead of him, he darted to the other side of the road. Avoiding who he could, he moved with purpose, a strong wind at his back.

Ghostward stretched out before him, a melting pot of sights and sounds. Late-night food vendors called out to passersby, their carts steaming in the cold. They sold giant pretzels slathered in mayo, dusted with smoked paprika, and little paper cups of roasted peanuts, tossed in a caramelized bird's eye chili glaze. Some carts boasted more artisanal treats: honey-drizzled figs skewered and wrapped in bacon or charred Padron peppers tossed with flaky salt and fresh herbs. A newspaper stand stood abandoned, plastic covers flapping. A fire engine roared past David, sirens screaming and flashing, going in the opposite direction. He knew where. The Midnight Laundromat. The Esternati Chapter House hidden below. His heart sank at the thought of his colleagues. But he couldn't back down now. He had a plan. He needed to set it in motion before it was too late. He picked up the pace.

Soon enough, the monolithic shape of Waldorf Tower loomed in the distance. Once the pride and joy of Ghostward, the building had been mostly forgotten by its citizens. Built as a stunning display of Art Deco architecture in the '40s, it had once been the site of affluent and tasteless parties for Ghostward's elite. Now, aged and decaying, it'd become an apartment building for those who enjoyed a unique style and middle-of-the-road mortgages. A jagged flash of lightening from above briefly illuminated the building's desolate parking lot. David crossed the concrete quickly, water splashing beneath his hurried steps. Reaching the tower's front entrance, he disappeared inside.

Once in the ancient, creaking elevator, David pressed the button for the fifth floor. His damp fingers left smudges on the archaic panel. The faint whirr of old machinery did little to mask the sound of his laboured breath. His reflection in the dull metal doors fragmented. His loose red tie and rolled up sleeves suggested a man both prepared and burdened by the weight of what lay ahead.

The elevator dinged. David stepped out and entered his apartment. The space inside was dark, lit only by the intermittent flashes outside. The cityscape, framed by large living room windows, greeted him as he arrived. It was a well-appointed home. The kind of place where someone could be quite comfortable. But the gloom, combined with the clutter of papers and books, suggested a life consumed by obsession.

David hung his coat on the rack by the door and tried to flatten the wrinkles across his white button-up, caused by the day's exertions. He let out a slow, steady sigh, then crossed the living room and moved through the door into his study.

The home office was ground zero for his disorganized research. Sheets of paper covered the surface of a sturdy oak desk. Most were scrawled with notes on the arcane and sketches of occult sigils. A cordless phone sat amidst them, beside a full ashtray. The bookshelves on either side of the entrance door were packed with tomes on magic and folklore, their spines worn, titles fading.

David picked up the phone from his desk and dialled.

"You've reached Jessie. Have at it."

The beep sounded; he inhaled sharply.

"Jessie… It's Dad. I know, I know, but please… hate me later. Right now, I need you to listen."

David leaned back against his desk, his free hand pinching the skin above his nose. Tired tears beaded in the corner of his eyes. He blinked them away.

"Our family has always been a magnet for darkness," he told her. "You know this. But after what happened… I–I wanted to shelter you kids. I wanted to hold back the tide."

Another stab of lightening filled the study with a dazzling flash. Standing again, David moved to a window on his right. Using his fingers to split the blinds, he peered out through the foggy glass and onto the street below. His signet ring grazed gently against the rigid synthetic slats. Outside, almost imperceptible in the shadows below, David could see a figure watching. The stalker's eyes glowed an unsettling green. The figure stood motionless, staring up at David's floor.

"But the dam I built had leaks, and now… it's about to break. I should've done better. Prepared you both for what's to come."

He turned away from the window, closing the door to the study. With the phone still tucked under his chin, he retrieved a nub of chalk from one of the bookshelves. On the inside of the entrance door, a series of symbols had been drawn within a half-completed circle. With the chalk gripped between his fingers, David leant forward and connected the final line. Now complete, the sigil irradiated faintly.

"Take care of Elijah," he continued. "He needs you. And find Lockart. She can help." He swallowed. "Trust no one else. Our enemies own the police."

David faltered, longing passing over his face. "I… I wish I could see you both again."

He chuckled softly,

"Finally take that holiday to Okinawa like your mom always wanted."

Muffled through the thin walls, David flinched as he heard the front door burst open. Its locks and chains shattered under the force of the intruder. A grim smile now tinged with fatalism formed.

"Hmm. Another life perhaps."

Heavy footsteps filled the hallway outside the study. David took a seat behind his desk. The phone still cradled to his ear, he withdrew a small pistol from one of the drawers and pointed it towards the living room in anticipation.

"I…" His words caught for a second in his throat as emotion threatened to overwhelm him. "I think I've come to believe that, doomed or not, one should always fight for a better world, my dear. We must *strive* to resist. In that, we can at least die human. Remain human. And perhaps, in some small way, our humanity lives on. Even after all of this… is gone."

The study door began to tremble violently. The glowing chalk sigil pulsed, resisting the pressure on the other side. Setting the phone down in front of him, David sniffled, wiping the salty moisture from his cheeks.

⊙⊙⊙

November 1st, 1996 – 11 AM

Jessie stood in the narrow doorway between her bathroom and the rest of her home. Her toothbrush, still coated in white foam, poked out from the corner of her mouth. She'd only just rolled out of bed. Her dreadlocked hair was a clumpy mess, a torn *Earth Crisis* t-shirt and a pair of black underpants covered her tired form. As she scrubbed her teeth, Jessie scanned the cluttered studio apartment with disdain. Dirty clothes and socks spilled out of an overturned laundry basket near the window. Wrappers from late-night takeout mingled with empty glass bottles, strewn across the carpet. A pile of dog-eared zines sat precariously atop a small bedside table. The latest from *Slug and Lettuce*, *Profane Existence*, *HeartattaCK*, and *Punk Planet*. On a wall-mounted shelf next to them, an impressive collection of cassette tapes surrounded a battered boombox and an old answering machine. The latter's small green light blinked insistently as the device played back her most recent message.

Jessie hadn't paid much attention at first. The faint crackle of static and muffled voices were white noise to her as she tried to shake off her hangover. But slowly, the words her father spoke began to sink in.

CRASH!

The sound was confusing – something breaking, something being forced open. A door? Jessie frowned. Slowly, she removed the toothbrush from her mouth, her heart thumping hard in her chest.

"Good to see you, Professor." This other voice was low, unplaceable. Dripping with menace.

"Hello -----..." This voice was her father's, but the name he used to greet the other was distorted. Obscured. A kind of non-sound rising up to swallow the word whole.

"Finally showing your face, I see," her father continued.

"So, you do recognize me. Even after all these years… Good," the voice oozed.

A cold knot twisted in Jessie's stomach as she leaned in towards the machine. She waited for her father's response. Instead, three loud gunshots exploded through the speaker. Jessie flinched as the room spun. Her fingers found the doorframe and tightened around it for support. The recording continued.

"I… I had to try," her father whispered.

"Yeah. You did."

There was a shout. Scuffling sounds of a brief struggle. Another crash, and then a final… *BEEP*

The silence that followed blared like guitar feedback in Jessie's mind. Her dad's words, resigned. Almost bitterly amused. He'd known the end was coming. He'd already made his peace.

Jessie gasped, realizing she'd been holding her breath. Her lungs shivered; a pulse thudded in her ears. She stared down at the toothbrush in one hand, a streak of the minty paste smeared across her knuckles. Her arms went slack, her face hardening into stone. The toothbrush slipped, landing mute on the carpet. She took a step and stumbled.

"What. The. Fuck…"

AL TABERN

y mensajes al 627 75 97 81

ROS - Murcia

12 ... Octubre

INTERLUDE

The Finger Lakes Region, August 1981…

The DeLuca lake house stood proud against a backdrop of shimmering water and lush greenery. Its modern design complimented the natural beauty surrounding it. A world away from the moody, rain-soaked climate of Ghostward, their holiday home afforded them a much-needed getaway at least once a year. A six-hour journey by plane, such trips were a rare indulgence. But when the frigid bustle of the city had them yearning for warm days and serene, star-filled nights, the lake house beckoned with an inviting embrace. In the driveway out front, a minivan was parked. Pressed against the inside of its rear windows, distorted cartoonish faces of blow-up pool toys waited for a turn in the sun.

A child's voice rang out from the backyard. "Get it, Jessie! Get it!"

Crouched at the edge of a small wooden pier, a young girl held a tree branch in her hands. A bright pink, uncooked hotdog had been skewered to its point, now dangling atop the water's surface. Even at six years old, Jessie's face was scrunched up with maturity beyond her years. She teased something beneath the reflective ripples. The wiener bobbed enticingly, drawing the attention of a large eel, swimming in hungry circles around the bait. The creature's sleek body gyrated with determination.

"Elijah! Stop jumping!" Jessie said to her brother as the branch dipped precariously close to the eel. Her brother bounced on the pier behind her, unable to contain his excitement.

Despite being born at the same time, Elijah was smaller than his sister. Skinny and pale, he displayed almost no signs of their Italian or Iranian heritage. Whereas Jessie was olive-skinned and healthy-looking, Elijah was a sickly child, already mired by years of health problems and bad dreams.

"Ewwww!" he said with a shriek. "It looks slippery!" He turned to a third child standing a few paces back. "Hey, Nathan! What do you reckon it feels like?"

Nine years old, a little chubby, with a slightly tanned complexion, Nathan crossed his arms as he watched his friend's game with a stern expression. "I dunno. A big worm probably." He shrugged dismissively, but a faint twinge of curiosity betrayed his otherwise stoic demeanour.

Jessie lifted the stick from the water. The wiener was gone. The eel had nibbled it free. She groaned as her mom's voice echoed across the hilly yard behind them.

"Jessie! Can you come here for a second?"

Thrusting the branch into Elijah's hands, she huffed to herself and stood. Leaving the boys behind, she began to make her way back to the house. "COMIIIING!"

Elijah's eyes grew bright as the branch lay in his fists. This newfound responsibility filled him with glee. "Yuss!"

While Elijah celebrated, Nathan bent down and grabbed another hot dog from the open packet beside them. Holding the tube of processed meat in his hand, he imagined it grilled – in a bun, with mustard and ketchup, its charred skin crackling, filling his nostrils with smoke and salt.

"Here, gimme that." He reached for the stick.

"No way, José!"

Nathan rolled his eyes. This whole game was starting to bug him. Why were they throwing perfectly good food away? His folks would never buy stuff like this. It was practically treasure! Like Elijah's dad, Nathan's was a professor, too. An anthropo-something-or-other. He was always telling stories about treasure – riches of a different kind. Gold and artefacts. Amulets and ancient scrolls. His wife, a Yazidi refugee from Kurdistan, was both the love of his life and the subject of his research. Together, they made a point to live traditionally, cutting out as many Americanized foods from their son's diet as possible. What they ate was meant to keep Nathan *"connected to your roots, darling! To your roots!"* But he hated it. Most nights, he was presented with steaming bowls of Kurdish biryani or warming lentil soups, while school mates dined on tv dinners and fast food orders. Nathan didn't mind the lamb Koftas or herby flatbreads – but they were for special occasions only.

For a long time, he'd not even been sure if the "Happy Meal" at McDonald's was real. There was a possibility Jessie had invented it in order to torment him. A STRONG possibility, he'd say. But this was partly why he enjoyed being around the twins – why he'd begged his folks to let him spend the summer holidays with them at the lake. They always had junk food! Ever since their first playdate a couple years ago, the DeLucas had provided him with a steady and secretive supply of sweet and salty snacks. On the way here, Nathan had fantasized about fried chicken, American barbeque, big bags of potato chips, sour candies, and of course… American hot dogs.

He looked at the floppy meat cylinder in his hand again, considering how much more exciting it'd been in his imagination.

This should be going in my mouth, he thought. *Not the water…*

But a DeLuca game was a DeLuca game. Once the twins had it in their minds to do something, there was no stopping them until they grew bored. And so, play he must. Darting forward, he attempted to snatch the branch from the younger boys' hand. When Elijah evaded, he fell on him, wrestling for control of the revered stick.

"Give it here!"

"Get them sticky fingers off!" Elijah replied through clenched teeth, jerking it away.

The two boys tumbled into a playful fight. Bare knees scraping against wooden planks. Their laughter and taunts, innocent and cheerful, drifted across the lake. Oblivious of the horror to come.

The first warning was from the lake itself. A ripple broke the surface, spreading out like a sinister omen, lapping against the pier's weathered structure.

"Let go!" Elijah snapped, yanking hard.

"Give me a turn, you little turd!" Nathan shot back.

A tall shape rose from the waters behind them. It emerged slowly, unnaturally, parting the surface with a whisper. As its shadow fell upon them both, blocking out the sun, Elijah froze, his hands still reaching for the stick. Something itched in the back of his mind. Déjà vu. Sickly fear. He'd lived this moment already, just… not here. Not in waking.

Elijah let his grip loosen. Grinning in unaware triumph, Nathan grabbed the branch, pulling it in and flattening it against his stomach. A short-lived victory. Something was off. Following Elijah's glassy gaze, he let the stick clatter in front of his knobbly knees.

The creature was humanoid, yet impossibly tall. As the boys' eyes tried to translate what they were seeing, its true nature became terrifyingly clear. Although it took the form of a man, it was, in fact, composed entirely of writhing eels. The very same kind as the one they had been teasing moments earlier. Putrid water cascaded down its broad shoulders, and a whiff of mud and rot wafted towards them.

They screamed.

Scrambling to his feet, his small legs pumping, bolting up the pier, towards the house, Elijah called out, "Jessie! Help!"

Nathan wasn't as quick. Still clambering to stand, he squealed as a sharp, searing pain jolted through his ankle. A massive eel, the size of a snake, shot from the creature's outstretched arm, latching onto him. Sharp, needle-like teeth sank into his flesh. It death-rolled, ripping through his skin and muscle, pumping hot blood across the pier like a renegade firework. Nathan screamed again.

"Eli! WAIT!"

Though he heard him, Elijah could not stop. Panic had overtaken him. Just like in his nightmares. Adrenaline powered his tiny body. He was no longer a kid, no longer a mind with thoughts or desires – just motion. Just movement. There wasn't room for anything else.

Halfway up the hill now, knees buckling, body collapsing. The world disappearing. Shock, overwhelming. Behind him, Nathan screamed again. There were more eels now, sliding and flapping across the pier, each wrapping around and engulfing his body, dragging him to the water. A single, terrified eye remained visible within the vortex of serpentine shapes. A tiny hand, reaching out, grasping…

grasping…

grasping…

Elijah lay motionless up ahead, barely conscious. A single, trembling word escaped.

"N-N-Nathan…"

AL TARENTIN [illegible]

y mensajes al 627 79 97 81

[illegible]ROS - Murcia

[illegible]zo 12 de Octubre

RE 22:0[illegible]

BE

THREE

Horizon Behavioural Clinic, November 8th, 1996, 7:30 AM

An early morning haze of grey hung over the city. The Horizon Behavioural Clinic stood modestly on the outskirts of Ghostward, cornered against the slopes of the Blackridge Range. The building's façade was unremarkable: an off-white stucco-finished structure, built in the late '80s. The clinic belonged somewhere else. Perhaps the dust-swept deserts of New Mexico, but not here.

Inside, Elijah DeLuca lay on a single bed in a dimly lit room. His thin physique curled beneath a tangle of sheets. His breathing rose and fell in shallow and uneven spasms. As he stirred, a soft, lazy movement rose from beneath his pillow. The phantom tail of a freshwater eel emerged, then vanished.

"NATHAN!"

Jolting himself awake, his scream erupted as a choke. His eyes darted wildly around the room, his pupils blown wide with terror. The early morning darkness seemed to ripple and shift around him, taking on monstrous forms. He could hear whispering, each voice taunting with incomprehensible murmurs. Remembering the nightmare, Elijah clutched his knees to his chest, rocking himself back and forth, trying to find grounding. Just like the therapists had told him to.

"It's n-not r-real..." he whimpered. "J-just a d-dream... j-just a d-dream..."

Outside in the hallway, Dr. Simon Fairbanks began his morning patrol. Fluorescent lights buzzed and flickered, reflecting against the polished, sterile linoleum floor. Pausing briefly by Elijah's room, he glanced through a small rectangular window. Inside, Elijah was a ball, tightly coiled at the head of his bed. His face hung limply in his hands. Making a note of it, the doctor continued towards the front of the clinic. Further down the corridor, a spluttering radio presenter ranted through the corridors.

"…and listen, folks, I'm telling you, it's all connected!" the excitable voice declared, dripping with conspiratorial fervour. *"The fire in Ghostward, the others in Istanbul, London, Tokyo… hell, even New Zealand for Christ's sake!"*

Dr. Fairbanks frowned. This was Sandra's doing. Her private interest in the wild accusations flung around on right-wing talk radio was well-known. But Fairbanks thought she kept it low-key at work. The woman was a nuisance – the daughter-in-law of the CEO, given a job she had no interest in doing and was terrible at. If somebody complained, they'd need to have a serious talk. Fairbanks dreaded what it might mean for his own career if he rocked the boat, but he couldn't just do nothing, could he? Adjusting his white coat with nervous tension, he continued into the reception area.

At the front desk, Sandra slouched in her chair, twirling the cord from the office phone around her fingers.

"Oh, well, I don't know about that," she said, her tone dismissive. "Justin has always been a little—"

Entering briskly, Dr. Fairbanks interrupted her mid-sentence. "Sandra," he said, "Ms. DeLuca will be here in an hour or so to collect Elijah. Can you please make sure someone gets him up and ready to go?"

Sandra rolled her eyes but gave him a cursory nod to show she understood. Clearly unimpressed by the urgency in his voice, she turned back and continued her conversation. Fairbank's felt his cheeks grow warm. He eyed her for a second, before his attention was once again drawn to the ridiculous conspiracy theorist blaring from the radio.

"Go ahead! Call me crazy," the man snarled. *"That's just what the globalists want! The fact of the matter is, these were SYSTEMATIC, COORDINATED, attacks!"* Fairbanks' gut sank a little. He considered with dread the possible sources for this man's crazy tirade. Then, deciding he really needed his morning coffee, he shook his head and turned on his heel, leaving the noise, and Sandra's bullshit, behind.

⊙⊙⊙

As the drizzle outside grew stronger, Jessie leaned back on the hood of her beat-to-shit Toyota. She balanced a cigarette between her fingers and watched the front doors through the veil of rain. The parking lot was still mostly empty. Aside from her car, only three other vehicles could be seen gliding through the low-hanging fog. Jessie exhaled a plume of smoke into the damp air and looked up at the rolling clouds. They looked hungry. Like a mouth. A yawning, carnivorous sky.

Thunder rumbled in the distance.

At last, movement from the clinic drew her back in. The front doors slid open and out stepped her brother. No longer in his medical gown, Elijah wore a pair of black skinny jeans and a black Deadguy tee, partially hidden by a green canvas jacket. He and Jessie had once spent an entire evening adorning that thing with a variety of patches. That had been two months before Elijah went to Horizon. A small travel bag hung jauntily over one of his shoulders. Jessie straightened, flicking her cigarette to the wet ground. She hopped down from her perch and strode towards him.

"Yo, little bro!" she called out, a teasing lilt in her voice.

Elijah groaned, his breath visible in the cold air. "We're th-the s-same a-ag—"

"Five minutes! I'm five minutes older." She reached out and hugged him.

Caught off-guard, Elijah stood awkwardly in her embrace. Slowly, his expression shifted to reluctant affection as he gave in. Wrapping his arms loosely around her, he could hear his heartbeat aligning itself with her own. The two years peeled away. Despite their troubles, an embrace from his twin always bought a modicum of peace.

"It's… good t-to see you," he admitted softly.

Jessie pulled back, her hands resting atop his shoulders. She examined his face. His dark hair hung thick and tangled across his forehead. Jessie grinned, flicking stray strands away from his eyes.

"You're a mess!"

"Doctor Fairbanks s-says I have t-to be back in the morning,"

"I know." Placing an arm around his shoulder, Jessie led her brother towards the car, giving him a reassuring squeeze as they reached it. "You ready?"

Thick droplets of water streaked down the outside of the windshield as they settled into their seats. With a turn of the ignition, the engine growled softly. Behind the wheel, Jessie glanced sideways at her brother. He sat next to her, fussing with his jacket zipper. Raising her eyebrow, she smiled again. Noticing her watching, Elijah stared back defiantly. *She looks exactly the same*, he thought. Dressed in her trademark red jeans, Doc Martens, black leather jacket. Only the t-shirt was different. Some new band he'd never heard of.

Refused.

"You…" Elijah began, tilting his head slightly and trying to make sense of the moment. "You d-don't look dressed for a funeral."

Jessie laughed and nudged him playfully. "Neither do you."

For the first time in a long time, the faintest trace of a smile came over him. In the quiet of the car, with the patter of rain filling the spaces between words and wounds, a peculiar sense of discovery blossomed inside. Like finding something long thought lost. A fleeting moment of normalcy, of clarity. It brought Elijah right back to the days when they were kids, playing Barbies in their parent's townhouse. He had to remind himself that had been another life. Only slightly more real than fiction. He reached into the bag at his feet and withdrew a blue inhaler. Puffing on it, he watched his sister as she put the car into reverse and pulled out of the parking space.

◉◉◉

The old wrought-iron gates of St. Lazarus Cemetery creaked faintly as mourners passed through them, their steps softened by a blanket of mouldering autumnal leaves. From the rolling grass, towering mausoleums and timeworn statues emerged, their shadows casting distorted inky black shapes on the ground. Preening itself with slow, deliberate motions, a crow kept watch from the outstretched arm of a crumbling stone angel.

A modest crowd stood around the newly dug plot, their dark umbrellas forming a mandala of black petals from above. Jessie and Elijah stood amongst them as emotions of grief and anger simmered beneath the surface.

Before them, a polished coffin perched above the open grave. Soon, it would be lowered into the earthy mire and forgotten. A priest stood at the head of the plot, his voice a steady and practiced cadence. A well-worn bible sat open in his hands as he read.

"For when the perishable puts on the imperishable, and the mortal puts on immortality, then shall come to pass..."

His words were like a TV with the volume turned down to three. Jessie found herself focusing instead on their father's casket. Her mind wandered, remembering the last time they'd spoken. An argument. About Elijah. About her. About everything really. And yet, in this moment, the details escaped her. The grudge held, though its reasoning had vanished. Next to her, Elijah tugged nervously at his sleeves, hunching his shoulders against the chill in the air. He looked smaller than she remembered. Two years at Horizon was supposed to help. They were supposed to give him the strength to face his demons, to become the person he really was. But as far as Jessie could tell, that time had stripped him bare – all his spark, his confidence, the sharp edges she knew and loved, seemed to have been dulled into nothing.

An older man with wire-rimmed glasses leaned towards her, his voice grating against the solemnity of the moment.

"Jessie? Jessie DeLuca? By god, you've grown up. I'm so sorry for your loss. Your... your father was a good man. I want you to know that. Of course, the university sends its condolences..."

Shoving her hands deep into her pockets, Jessie clenched, then opened, then clenched again. The old man was a pebble in her shoe. Small, but unrelenting.

"...organizing all this was the least they could do, if you ask me..." the man continued with a mixture of pride and pity.

"Quiet!" the priest snapped as he cast a disapproving look their way. The old man recoiled in embarrassment and Jessie smiled. A man of God. Good for something after all.

Returning to his reading, the priest's voice rose slowly with conviction. "Then shall come to pass the saying: O' death, where is your victory? O' death, where is your sting?"

Elijah fidgeted beside her. She side-eyed him, noting the sheen of rain in his hair and the way he avoided looking directly at the grave. She wanted to say something to him, but whatever those words were, whatever it was that could make this moment right, refused to come.

The cemetery stretched out long, tombstones disappearing into the mist. The rain was light, but the cold seeped through her clothes. It settled on her bones.

After the priest's lecture was finished and their father placed in the ground, Jessie found refuge behind a gnarled walnut tree near her car. Leaning softly against the trunk, she pressed another cigarette to her lips and sighed. The mourners – her father's colleagues – were finally leaving. They'd each drive home. Spend time with their families. Share meals and decry the injustice of another soul taken too soon. How fucking lame. They hadn't known her father – not really. If they had, they'd get it. They'd understand why Jessie couldn't afford the luxury of grief – or closure. No. It simply wasn't in the cards. She needed to tell Elijah what she knew. Play him what she'd heard. But how? Watching the procession leave, she took one last drag and stubbed the butt out on a knot in the tree.

"There you are," Elijah's voice cut through her, sending her into a minor panic as she realized the moment to share had come. He approached hesitantly, dwarfed by the foliage around them.

"Th-thought y-you'd quit," he said, noticing the steaming cigarette at her feet. "Or gone s-straight edge or something."

Jessie swallowed. Pulling a portable tape player from her pocket, she held it up for him to see. "You need to hear this."

Elijah frowned. A second later, their father's voice crackled to life. Tinny. Distorted. But unmistakably his.

"Jessie. It's Dad. I know, I know, but please… hate me later. Right now, I need you to listen…"

"W-wait, he–he c-called you?"

"Shh!" she cut him off, her focus trained on the tape, searching frantically for some secret, a hidden answer she'd so far missed.

The seconds passed sluggishly as the recording played on, finishing just as unceremoniously as she'd remembered. Jessie now sat on her car hood with folded arms. In front of her, Elijah grew more and more erratic as he paced, running his fingers through his tangled mop. He found tangled clumps, tugging on them, using the pain to tether him to reality.

"Murdered?" he finally blurted out. "No! Th-the police r-ruled it a suicide!"

"Dad said not to trust them." The words felt heavy in her mouth.

Elijah spun to face her, throwing his arms up. "Then what?" he demanded.

Jessie stood, flicking open her Zippo to spark yet *another* cigarette, the flame briefly revealing her determination. "We do our own digging."

Elijah groaned, his hands now dragging down his cheeks, pulling on the dark bags beneath his eyes. "Ugh, what?"

"Check his apartment. The old man has to have left some sort of clue."

"A clue?" Elijah echoed, his pacing resuming. "Jessie! This isn't a g-g-game! If you're r-right, then it's dangerous! I h-have to be b-back at the clinic soon! And besides, didn't D-Dad just say we need t-to g-go into hiding?"

"Honestly, fuck him. I ain't living under some rock just because he says so. Are you?"

"I've already been living under a rock," Elijah replied. "You two put me there."

Hearing those words, Jessie's jaw clenched. Her eyes narrowed. A bitter taste spread across her tongue. But then, seeing Elijah, watching as he turned, as his shoulders sagged in retreat, she let the anger evaporate. He was right. They had. All the good that'd done him. And yet, he wanted to go back. He was afraid, she realized. Perhaps for good reason.

"Murdered? N-no! No, no, no!" His pleading continued, growing softer and softer until silent. There were tears in his eyes when he said, "Our dad was an asshole, right? We don't owe him sh-shit."

Leaping up, Jessie pulled him in, holding him in a fierce embrace. "No," she said softly. "But we do owe her."

Elijah went limp in her arms. With those words came old memories. Fond ones, but also the kind that could beat you bloody.

"What would Mom want?"

3:30 PM, Across Town…

Waldorf Tower's tenant parking stretched around them; its expanse dotted with slumbering cars. Jessie pulled her Toyota in, parking at the very center. Her headlights cut through the darkness of late afternoon. The sound of wipers scraped against her windshield as thunder roared overhead.

"Jessie…" Elijah broke the long drive's silence, his fingers drumming anxiously against his knee. "You sure a-about this?"

Jessie peered up at the building ahead. "There's no doubt about it," she said. "Dad kept secrets from us. Secrets that got him killed."

Elijah leant forward in his seat to follow her gaze, his belt buckle seizing up.

"I d-don't get it," he mused, more to himself than her. "He was just a college professor. Teaching folklore to d-d— To d—" He paused, closing his eyes, trying to settle his words. "To *D&D* nerds, right?" He laughed, then frowned. "Who'd wanna k-kill him?"

Girded on all sides by the storm, the Art Deco styling of Waldorf Tower lent it the air of a powerful sentinel. Resolute and declaring victory. When Jessie next spoke, her voice was firm. "Well, if we're gonna find any answers, they're up there."

The car doors groaned, letting in the cold. Jessie stepped out first, the hood of her jacket pulled up in defence against the deluge. Across from her, Elijah joined. He bristled in the wind.

Waldorf Tower eclipsed them both, its peak disappearing into the clouds above. A bolt of electricity snapped loudly, exposing it in sharp relief. And then… the sky shifted. Just for a moment, the rain recoiled, and the heavens opened.

Above the building, a monstrous form revealed itself. A blasphemous shadow-puppet previously hidden behind the billowing clouds. A gargantuan entity, floating there, beyond the veil of reality, rippling with otherworldly power. Hundreds of beady eyes, burning green with malevolence, glared upon Ghostward. A gaping maw stretched wide. Teeth like needles, glistening with venom and viscous saliva. Thick, hostile feelers, scaley and dense, whipped and twirled in anguished orbit. An unholy wound in the fabric of the sky.

Elijah's mouth went dry. The hairs on his neck stood on end. He blinked. As suddenly as it had appeared, the entity was gone. Glancing over at his sister, he watched her wipe a stream of rainwater from her forehead. She hadn't seen it. It was his goddamn mind. All in his head. Again. Despair threatened to take him, just like it had years ago, but he balled his fists, shaking the vision off.

"Alright. Time to kick the hornet's nest," he heard himself say.

"Just like old times, huh?"

With the rain belting against their backs, the siblings approached the tower. As they neared, Jessie's lungs contracted in short, shallow gasps. Beside her, Elijah clenched his jaw, biting down hard on the inside of his cheek, letting the taste of copper soothe his machine-gun heart. Above them, the sky over Ghostward was a bruise, swollen and dark, bleeding heavily across the horizon…

To Be Continued…

One of the sole-survivors of the terrorist attack on Ghostward's Ester nati Chapter House, Sam Lockart is both studious and tough. Raised in the Esternati Order, she quickly rose through its ranks and became the prodigy of David DeLuca, it's last Compatriota (leader.) Hoping to honor her former mentor's wishes, Sam is determined to survive her plight and aid his children, Jessie and Elijah in this new, terrifying world they now find themselves in.

Future co-founder of the FBP, Jessie is a young woman with an axe to grind. Twin sister to Elijah, she is the more direct of the two, but also less emotionally available. She cares deeply for her brother and sees herself as his protector – whether he likes it or not! Jessie joined the local hardcore scene in her teens She was part of the original line-up for THE OUTRAGE, but after a failed romance with its vocalist, Hunter Garcia, she opted to leave and do her own thing.

Lead singer of the Outrage, and an old friend of Jessie and Elijah, Hunter is a young Colombian man who immigrated to Ghostward after spending his childhood in New Zealand. A bit of a blunt object, Hunter hits hard and asks questions later. He may look tough and unapproachable, but is a big softy at heart, and a romantic to boot. Despite the upsetting ending to his relationship with Jessie, Hunter still harbours feelings for her and is hopeful of a second chance one day.

Future co-founder of the Far Body Punks, Elijah is a troubled young man with a nervous disposition and a persistent stutter. Twin brother to Jessie, Elijah is the more emotionally vulnerable of the two. He doesn't know it yet, but Elijah is far more attuned to the supernatural than most. With no one to explain this to him, he has suffered over many years with what he perceived to be severe mental health issues.

BOOK 2:
ASTRAL PUNK